SCAREDY CATS

For Nikki Cave

Find out more about the Scaredy Cats
at Shoo's fabulous website:
www.shoo-rayner.co.uk

ORCHARD BOOKS
96 Leonard Street, London EC2A 4XD
Orchard Books Australia
32/45-51 Huntley Street, Alexandria, NSW 2015
First published in Great Britain in 2004
First paperback edition 2005
Copyright © Shoo Rayner 2004
The right of Shoo Rayner to be identified as the author
and illustrator of this work has been asserted by him in
accordance with the Copyright, Designs, and Patents Act, 1988.
A CIP catalogue record for this book is available
from the British Library.
ISBN 1 84362 441 9 (hardback)
ISBN 1 84362 730 2 (paperback)
1 3 5 7 9 10 8 6 4 2 (hardback)
1 3 5 7 9 10 8 6 4 2 (paperback)
Printed in Great Britain

Foggy Moggy Inn

Shoo Rayner

ORCHARD BOOKS

Inky was sneaking through the back
yard of the hotel where he lived, when
the sky seemed to crash down on him.

Inky's back arched in terror. He shot out of the gate, across the road, under a fence and over the fields.

He didn't stop until he got to the secret circle and joined the eight cats that waited for him. They were the other members of the secret society of Scaredy Cats.

"What was that terrible noise?"
Molly asked.

"They're putting new heating in the
hotel," Inky panted. "I tripped on
some copper pipes and they fell!"

"You dropped a clanger there, then!" said Max.

Inky sighed and the group laughed.

"You have to be careful when you're heating a hotel," growled Kipling.

Silence fell upon the secret circle. Kipling's eyes narrowed into slits. He was ready to tell a story. The story they had all come to hear.

"This story happened to my cousin Ollie," Kipling began. "His owner, Sally, was moving to a new house far away.

She strapped Ollie's basket to the
front seat of the car so that he could
see out of the window and they set off.

The journey went quickly, but as they neared the end, they had to travel across a high, lonely moor. It was getting dark when they began the climb uphill.

Ghostly fingers of mist swirled over the windscreen. They seemed to be looking for a way into the car.

The mist grew thicker and turned into a dense fog.

The cats' eyes in the middle of the road could hardly be seen. Sally inched the car from one twinkling cat's eye to another. Ollie watched mesmerised.

Then, suddenly, there were no more cats' eyes...and the car engine died.

Sally turned the key again and again. The starter motor shrieked in the darkness, but the engine would not come back to life.

The fog made the silence cold and eerie. Sally switched on her mobile phone. The screen cast a weird green glow on her face.

"Oh no!" she looked at Ollie and
sighed. "There's no phone signal here."

The mist parted and a pale light
caught Ollie's eye. He stared hard,
trying to make Sally look too.

"Ollie! There's a light," Sally gasped.
"Let's hope it's a house. We can phone
for help."

Carrying Ollie in the basket, Sally stumbled towards the light. The fog clung to them. The damp, soaking air caught in the back of their throats. It tasted old and stale.

"I don't believe it!" Sally exclaimed,
as she read a sign over the door.
"Foggy Moggy Inn... Ollie! It's a hotel!"

22

Inside, a log fire crackled and the glowing candlelight made the place warm and cosy. It was a homely, real old-fashioned country inn.

A tiny white-haired old lady greeted them. "Hello, I'm Mrs Walker." She spoke with a thin reedy voice. "We weren't expecting any guests tonight."

She smiled and spoke to Ollie in the
basket. "Aren't you the Foggy Moggy
tonight!"

Mrs Walker looked confused when Sally explained about the car and asked if she could use the inn's phone.

"No one should be out in this weather," Mrs Walker said, her eyes glinting. "You'd better stay the night."

Soon they were chatting in the
kitchen as Sally ate her supper.

Ollie wasn't happy. Mrs Walker looked like a sweet old lady, but something about her made his back arch and his fur bristle.

There was no electricity in the place.
Sally's bedroom had its own log fire
and a jug of water with a bowl.

"It's like a time warp here!" Sally said to Ollie, blowing her candle out and settling down to sleep.

Ollie still wasn't happy. He kept a
watchful eye open. He could sense
that something was wrong.

In the warmth of the fire, though, Ollie was soon fast asleep.

The burning logs shifted. With a flurry of sparks, a flaming log fell out of the fire and rolled onto the carpet.

The heat woke Ollie. He leaped onto
Sally's bed and wailed in her ear.

By the time Sally opened her eyes and understood what was happening, the fire had already spread. They were trapped!

Hot smoke filled their lungs. Ollie ran to the window but it was jammed tight. Sally followed and hammered at the handle with her fists, but it just wouldn't budge.

As terror gripped her, Sally hurled a chair at the window. The glass shattered into thousands of pieces. Ollie led the way out onto the roof below the window and Sally followed.

Giant flames lunged at them but,
with one giant leap, they escaped and
landed safely on the ground.

The inn was ablaze. There was nothing they could do. Ollie looked for Mrs Walker's face at a window, but all he could see was the cat on the inn sign. Its eyes glowed red as the flames took hold.

Sally and Ollie found their way back to the car and waited for daylight. The fire died down and the fog closed in. They felt very lonely.

When they woke, the sun was shining and a postman was tapping on the window. "Are you all right?" he asked.

When Sally told him about their near escape, the postman looked puzzled.

"There was an inn round here once," he told her. "But the stories say it burned down years ago!"

Ollie and Sally searched but there was no sign of where the inn had stood the night before. No ashes, just weeds and brambles.

"People have gone missing round here before," the postman told her. He pointed at Ollie, "I reckon your moggy saved your life last night!"

Ollie couldn't wait to get away from that terrible place.

Strangely, the car started first time!"

The Scaredy Cats stared, wide-eyed, at Kipling. The silence was shattered by a tremendous crash.

"Inky!" Crang! "Inky!" Blong! Bedang!
"Time for me to go," said Inky.

"It's going to be cold tonight," said
Kipling. "I hope your owners won't
be lighting any log fires."

Inky looked across at the hotel
and shivered.

A thin wisp of smoke was drifting
from the chimney...

SCAREDY CATS

Shoo Rayner

❏ Frankatstein	1 84362 729 9	£3.99
❏ Foggy Moggy Inn	1 84362 730 2	£3.99
❏ Catula	1 84362 731 0	£3.99
❏ Catkin Farm	1 84362 732 9	£3.99
❏ Bluebeard's Cat	1 84362 733 7	£3.99
❏ The Killer Catflap	1 84362 744 2	£3.99
❏ Dr Catkyll and Mr Hyde	1 84362 745 0	£3.99
❏ Catnapped	1 84362 746 9	£3.99

Little HORRORS

❏ The Swamp Man	1 84121 646 1	£3.99
❏ The Pumpkin Man	1 84121 644 5	£3.99
❏ The Spider Man	1 84121 648 8	£3.99
❏ The Sand Man	1 84121 650 X	£3.99
❏ The Shadow Man	1 84362 021 X	£3.99
❏ The Bone Man	1 84362 010 3	£3.99
❏ The Snow Man	1 84362 009 X	£3.99
❏ The Bogey Man	1 84362 011 1	£3.99

These books are available from all good bookshops,
or can be ordered direct from the publisher:
Orchard Books, PO BOX 29, Douglas IM99 1BQ
Credit card orders please telephone 01624 836000 or fax 01624 837033
or e-mail: bookshop@enterprise.net for details.

To order please quote title, author and ISBN and your full name and address.
Cheques and postal orders should be made payable to 'Bookpost plc'.
Postage and packing is FREE within the UK
(overseas customers should add £1.00 per book).

Prices and availability are subject to change.